*Henrietta P. Hoppenbeek
would like to dedicate this book to
Rosalind Price.
May your explorification
be wide and wonderful.*

Henrietta gets a letter

Here I am.

2

This is me. I'm Henrietta.

Dad says there's no one better, but that's because he loves me. Kings and queens and angels probably are better.

Also, animals who don't bite are very good. I don't bite, not unless you happen to be a chocolate ripple cake.

Here's Albert. He's my brother and he hasn't learnt to poo in the loo yet.

Here is Mum and Dad,

and Madge,
our fat
brown dog,

and Grannie who
wears gumboots,
and Grampa who
gives prickly kisses

and
Olive Higgie,
my best friend,

and
cousin Edgar
who draws
pictures
of cars,

and Aunt Lulu
who was once
in a circus.

Uncle George is meant to be here but Mum says,
'No doubt he has slept in.'

Uncle George is a scallywag, which means
he is sometimes getting into trouble.

We're having a party for Albert because he is two.

Here's the birthday cake.
Lordy Lordy, it's chocolate ripple cake.
I can hardly stop myself from biting it.
Everybody sings Happy Birthday Albert.
Lucky Albert.
Everybody has a piece of cake except Madge,
because she's a greedy-guts with a fat tummy.

Albert's piece is bigger than mine.

I'm absolutely sure it is.

'That's not fair!' I say loudly,

because it's important to let everyone know

when there has been an injustice.

'Albert's piece is bigger than mine!'

'That's because it's his birthday,' says Mum.

Dad says,

'You'll get the biggest piece on your birthday.'

Aunt Lulu says,

'Don't worry, too much cake will give you spots.'

Olive Higgie looks alarmed,

but Grannie pats her on the wrist and says,

'Lulu is just teasing.'

I'm cross.

Very, very cross. I can't wait till it's *my* birthday.

Albert has smeared his BIG piece of cake all over his face. And he has a new train.

I can't bear it. I fold my arms and sink into a huff. No one notices. Then I frown as hard as I can. Still no one notices. Then I snort and kick the table leg about fifty times.

Mum says, 'Henrietta, please stop kicking the table, it's driving me mad.'

So I stomp off to my room, slam the door, throw myself on the bed and wail.

No one comes. Not even Olive Higgie, my best friend. I stop wailing because I'm too busy thinking how unfair it is that I'm stuck in my room missing out on the party when everyone else is having a nice time without me.

The more I think about it, the crosser I get, and the crosser I get, the more I think there is only one thing left to do.

I explode into fifty billion pieces of Henrietta.

Not really. I try very hard to explode but nothing happens except a slight ache in my head. So I lie on the floor next to my corduroy donkey and give up on being cross. I try to think of things like outer space and puppies, and then I hear a

STRANGE
and
OMINOUS

scuffling noise under my bed. What could it be? Before I have time to investigate, Uncle George bursts into my room wearing a hat and singing, 'Don't let me be lonely, come dance with me, oh dance with me...'

'Uncle George, you're very late
and you missed out on cake.'

'Good. I don't care for cake.'

And I say,
'Well, neither do I, actually.'

And he says,
'Oh really? How very
grown up. So what
do you care for?'

'Lots of things. For
instance, Olive Higgie,
and my dog Madge,
but today I don't
particularly care for Albert.'

And he says,
'Well, I care very much
for the lovely
Miss Lily Fantuzzi,
the local librarian.'

I roll my eyes at this.

Then he says, 'I like to wear a hat, for no reason,
and to give something to someone else,
even a small thing.'
And I say, 'Me too.
I do drawings for Grannie.
She sticks them on her fridge.'
And he says,
'Well, I particularly like
to dance at a party.'
'Me too.'
'Oh, but I like to dance
with a good dancing partner.'
And I say, 'Me too,
only the very very finest.'
And then he takes me by the hand,
as if I was a ballerina,
and we go into the lounge room
and he bows and takes off his hat.
'Can we please have some music?
Henrietta and I would very much care to dance.'

We look very swish because Uncle George is always
dancing with the ladies, so he knows all the moves.

And I forget all about the cake and getting cross
because there are much better things to care about.

Like cuddles with Mum, for example.

And also investigating

STRANGE and OMINOUS noises...

Under the bed

Now it's night-time and the moon is out. I'm meant to be in bed, but I'm sitting on the floor having serious thoughts. Serious thoughts sometimes make you feel bad, whereas splendid thoughts always make you feel good. But sometimes there are serious thoughts that just have to be thought about – there's no way around or over or under it.

For instance, I absolutely cannot get into bed until I work out what made that

OMINOUS
and
STRANGE

noise I heard.

I don't think it's a crocodile, because crocodiles like to sit up and have tea and strawberry cupcakes. They don't want to slob around under a bed.

I don't think it could be a rhino, because rhinos prefer to point their horns in a threatening manner.

And if it was an elephant, the bed would look like this:

squashed

It might just be a monster, but I've heard that monsters lurk around in dark misty lakes eating dark misty lake bugs. So it's unlikely to be a monster. Very unlikely.

What *is* under my bed?

It might just be the kind of thing that likes to bite little girls' legs. And if it is, Dad should have a look under the bed, because you can't be a biter of dad legs *and* little girl legs. That's two different things.

'Dad!'

Dad pokes his head in the door.

'There's a scruffly something under my bed,'
So Dad slouches down under the bed. 'Have a good
look, Dad. It could be hiding.'

'I see one red crayon, one striped sock, a pair of
pyjama pants, a corduroy donkey and
a piece of Lego,

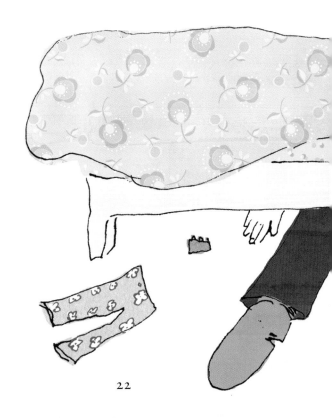

but there's not one single monster under this bed. Anyway, monsters are vegetarian,' he says.

'I know that. They only eat spinach and dark misty lake bugs, if you really want to know.'

Dad says, 'Is that so? I bet they'd prefer Albert's last piece of chocolate ripple cake!' And he growls like a monster and pretends to eat my foot.

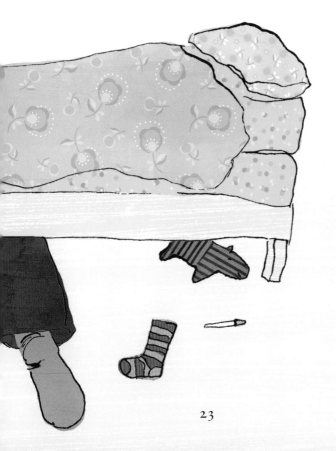

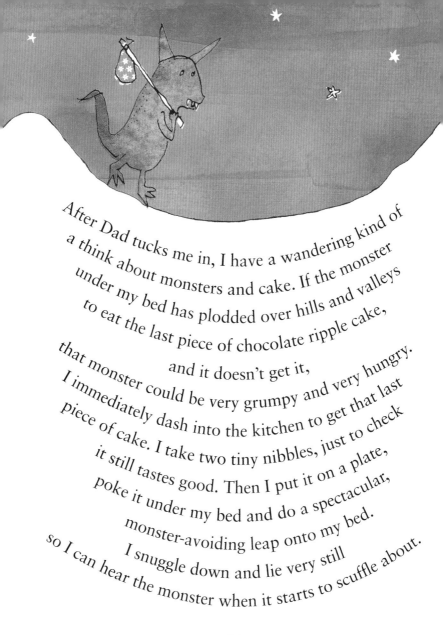

After Dad tucks me in, I have a wandering kind of
a think about monsters and cake. If the monster
under my bed has plodded over hills and valleys
to eat the last piece of chocolate ripple cake,
and it doesn't get it,
that monster could be very grumpy and very hungry.
I immediately dash into the kitchen to get that last
piece of cake. I take two tiny nibbles, just to check
it still tastes good. Then I put it on a plate,
poke it under my bed and do a spectacular,
monster-avoiding leap onto my bed.
I snuggle down and lie very still
so I can hear the monster when it starts to scuffle about.

The pickle trap

When I wake up, I immediately leap again, in a spectacular monster-avoiding way, and quickly check the cake. Oh Lordy Lordy, the cake has been eaten!

Not only that, there's a small silver key sitting right where the cake was.

Now I'm absolutely sure monsters don't have keys, because they live in lakes or forests or caves, and none of these places have doors that need to be locked.

So who ate the cake under my bed?

And what is the key for?

I'll have to ring Olive Higgie, code name O.H., second-in-charge and sharer-of-all-mysteries.

'O.H.,' I say. 'What hides under a bed, eats chocolate ripple cake and owns a small silver key?'

O.H. says,
'That's a hard question.
Do you have an easier one?'

I say,
'Not right now.
This is urgent.
There's something
under my bed. It
could be dangerous.'

O.H. says,
'We should feed it some pickles.'

'I don't think so. I think we need to set a trap.
A very clever, tricky kind of a trap.
I have a feeling this is a clever,
tricky kind of creature.'

O.H. says,
'Exactly! That's why pickles should
be part of the trap because
only very clever and tricky
kinds of creatures like them.'

I'm not so sure, but I don't want a disagreement. Some things are worth causing a bit of bother about, like chocolate ripple cake, or true love and bruises, but not pickles.

So after a lot of thinking and thinking, and a bit of laughing and jumping and creeping and acting like monsters, this is what we come up with:

the pickle trap

'What will you do, once it's trapped?' says O.H. 'I mean, what if it has sharp gnashing teeth and a long thrashing tail and huge grasping claws? And what if it's very, very angry at you for trapping it with a pickle?'

'Well, if that's the case,' I say, 'I'll just have to draw on my extraterrestrial courage and intelligence, as always.' But of course what I really plan to do is run and jump on Mum and Dad's bed, and yell HELP all the way there.

Night-time

When Mum tucks me into bed, she says,
'Henrietta, tell me,
why is there
a pickle
on a plate
on the floor?'

'It's a trap to catch the creature under my bed.'
'What an excellent idea,' she says.

And then she laughs, and so I laugh. It's splendid
to laugh, but it's tiring to feel splendid, so I drift off
to sleep and dream that Uncle George is eating
pickles with a rhino and I'm hiding behind a palm
tree just in case the rhino is in a mood for charging.
So I'm being quiet, quiet, quiet, when…

TING A LING A LING A LING

The bell rings right in my ear. I almost jump out of
the bed in fright and sheezamageeza
you won't believe what I see.

It's not a monster or a crocodile or a rhino
or an elephant. It's a very tiny person with wings.
And she's laughing.

'It's rude to laugh,' I say.

'Oops, is it? I thought it was very good to laugh,'
she says.

'Hmmmph,' I say.

'Well, most of the time it *is* good to laugh,
but not when someone nearly has a heart attack
because a bell has been rung in their ear.'

'Well,' she says, putting her hands on her hips.
'It's also rude to try to trap a fairy with pickles
when everyone knows chocolate is much nicer
than pickles.'

'Lordy Lordy,' I say. 'Are you a fairy?'

'I'm Mabel
May Hissop.
Born in the moonlight
and raised in a
pale orange poppy.
I prefer to fly freestyle,
and I cry milk tears.
I like mulberries, cherries
and chewy goop.
I don't like boiled eggs,
barking dogs or bossy boots.
My best friend is Aldo
and he's a swift.
Who are you?'

'I'm Henrietta the great go-getter.
I like chocolate ripple cake and cuddles.
I don't like pickles or whingers,
and I plan to be Queen one day.
I've been to the Wide Wide
Long Cool Coast of the Lost Socks.
Have you?'

'No, but I've visited the
Great Golden Palace
of the Queen Bee, and journeyed
on a breeze. Have you done that?'

'No, but I've climbed an apple tree
and waited in the leaves.'

'What did you wait for?'

'For nothing. I just sat
there because it was nice
next to the leaves.'

'Very good. I'm impressed,'
says Mabel. 'I knew I chose
the right sock to sleep in.'

'Have you been sleeping in my sock?'

Mabel darts under the bed, drags out my
red striped sock and wriggles inside.

'Yes, and I'm very tired now, so go back to bed
and I'll tell you the plan in the morning.'

'Plan? What plan?' I say,
but Mabel seems to
have fallen asleep.

To tell you the truth, I'm not used to fairies sleeping in my sock and I prefer to make up my own plans. In fact, I'm a great maker-upperer of plans and a great asker-of-questions.

I have a whole head full of questions for Mabel. While I'm thinking, Mabel calls out, 'Oody oody, please stop thinking so loudly. If you have questions, write them down and I'll answer them in the morning.'

So I quickly write my questions and then, even though I intend to stay awake all night just to keep an eye on Mabel May Hissop, I fall instantly asleep.

When I wake up, the sun is already beaming in the window. Mabel is still fast asleep in my sock and a little breeze puffs my list of questions right onto my lap.

Magic, I think to myself. There's magic in the air. There must be, because now all the questions have been answered.

Henrietta's list of questions

Where do fairies sleep?

Wherever they want to. Under oak leaves, in tree hollows, on clouds, in hammocks hanging from stars. I have a friend who sleeps on a spider web. I prefer to be under flowerpots on a bed of rose petals. But certain types of fairies like to sleep up high, in abandoned bird nests or chimney pots or peg baskets on washing lines.

What do fairies do during the day?

Sing songs, fly around, dance, smell flowers, do somersaults, make friends, chatter and snooze.

Can you make wishes come true?

Yes, sometimes. You have to practise. Once I turned Aldo into a worm by mistake. He was very grumpy about that.

do you have a mother or a father or
a brother or a sister?

No, all fairies belong to the same
family. There are no parents and no
children. If a fairy needs advice
there are wizards and other wise
creatures who can tell you useful
things.

are there boy fairies?

No, there are elves who are boys.

can you talk to dogs or horses or worms?

Worms don't speak. I can talk dog and
horse and bird and cat and cow, though
cows don't usually have much to say.

do you whinge?

Never. Whingeing is bad for your
voice and all fairies like to sing.

who is the boss of all fairies?
Me. Not Really. Everyone only bosses
themselves. It's against fairy law to
boss anyone but yourself.

do you get cross?
Getting cross makes your heart feeble.
But everyone gets cross sometimes, even
wizards and worms. Fairies try to get their
crossness out of their hearts quickly, and
then they sing a song or do a dance to
put the good feelings back in their
heart again.

what's the silver key for?
I'm not telling yet.

do fairies fall in love and get married?
Fairies are very good at falling in
love but not very good at getting
married.

is there anything else I should know?

My favourite colour is green. I am most well known for inventing the flying freestyle loop. My favourite dance is the lady bug boogie. It's impossible to trap a fairy but very good luck to have one under your bed. The best way to wake up a fairy is to tickle her toes with a feather while singing a dreamy kind of song.

Hmm, I think to myself, how do you tickle the toes of a fairy when the fairy is inside a sock? Exactly as I am pondering this, more writing appears on the paper:

If a fairy is sleeping in a sock and her toes aren't available for tickling, then tickle her cheeks instead.

Luckily I happen to have a collection of feathers in a box. But when I tickle Mabel's cheek, she opens one eye and not the other.

She whispers, 'Please sing. It's terrible to be woken up without singing.' And then she closes her eye and goes back to sleep.

I sing Uncle George's favourite song. 'You are my sunshine, my only sunshine. You make me happy when pies are gay...'

Suddenly Mabel's wings begin to twitch and then she wriggles out, wide awake.

'That's better,' she says. 'But when are pies gay?' Before I can find an answer she says, 'Always, I suppose, especially if they are made of mulberries.' Then she starts springing up and down, up and down like a yoyo, puffing. 'Excuse my jumping, it's my morning exercises.'

Now that it's light, I can see Mabel better. If you stood her next to a dandelion, she'd be just as tall but not as thin. She's wearing white stockings, with a hole where her big toe pokes through.

She has a laughing, grinning, sparkling face.
It makes me grin too, and then I start jumping
up and down. So we are jumping together.

'Is this magic?' I say.

Mabel says, 'If you think so, then it is.'

'Mabel, you are the first fairy I have ever jumped
up and down with, and this is the first magic
I've ever felt.'

Mabel says, 'I'm sure you have felt magic before. You just didn't know what it was.' She floats down and sits on my corduroy donkey. 'Any more

questions?'

'Yes. Why are you sleeping in my sock under my bed?'

'Good question. I have a problem, of course, and I need someone to help me.' I feel a bit special when Mabel says this.

'So, what's your problem?' I say, just like a good doctor.

'I've fallen in love with Bendle Bristlemouth, the naughty Elf of Endgarden. But Bendle has not yet fallen in love with me.'

'Drats,' says I, sympathetically. I intend to fall in love with a boy who has good ideas and a lion-heart who loves me back. I don't know how I can help Mabel, because I'm not yet a love expert.

'You can help me,' says Mabel. Right then I realise that Mabel can hear my thoughts.

'Bendle is a very charming elf, and all the fairies fall in love with him. In fact, he's just like your Uncle George. So, the plan is for you to find out what impresses Uncle George the most. I mean, what exactly should a lady do to make him fall in love with her?'

'Mabel,' I say in a serious tone, 'you do realise that Uncle George is a scallywag, don't you?'

'Of course I do. Fairies are always fond of scallywags, because somewhere in the very distant past we are slightly, very slightly, related to the Scallywag family.'

'Mabel,' I say in a thoughtful tone, 'why don't you ask Uncle George yourself?'

'Because grown-ups can't see or hear fairies. It's only possible to see something if you believe in it. Which is why the more things you believe in, the bigger the world becomes.'

'Mabel,' I say knowingly, 'that's very true and I intend to have the biggest possible world ever.'

'And do you intend to tidy up that world?' says my mum, who has just walked in with Albert on her hip.

Obviously she can't see Mabel, because she ignores her completely and gives me a kiss and says there's porridge for breakfast, and afterwards she and I are going to tidy up my room. Albert points a grubby finger at Mabel, who is laughing and flying out the window into the wide blue air.

Drats. I'd rather fly
out my window
than tidy my room.

The hat plan

Here I am with O.H.
in the garden.

O.H. is looking for Mabel under leaves and
inside flowers, but I have a feeling Mabel
will only be found if Mabel wants to be found,
so I'm only half looking and half thinking.

'Here's an acorn lid. Maybe Mabel can wear
it as a hat?' says O.H.

'It's funny you speak about hats, O.H.,
because I've been hatching a hat plan.'

'A hat plan?'

'Yes. You see, Uncle George always likes a hat and I thought we could make a hat that's tall enough to fit Mabel inside, so she can listen while we ask him about what makes him fall in love.'

'Excellent plot!' says O.H.

We're both pleased because it's a fine thing to hatch a secret plan.

Once the hat is finished
and O.H. has gone home,
I try it on Albert.
Then I try a question on Dad,
since Mum is at a yoga class.
'Dad, why do you love Mum?'
Dad, who's chopping
cabbage for soup, says,
'Well, I love your mum
because I just do.
Just like you love her.'
I say, 'No no. I mean why did you fall in love
with Mum and not the other ladies?'
Dad laughs, 'Well, because she was lovely. And
because she was a good dancer and a terrible cook.
And also I liked the confused look
in her eyes when she tried to sew.'
'Hmmmmm,' I say.
I'm not sure if this will be
helpful information
for Mabel or not.

48

Night-time again

Before I go to bed, I write a note.

dear Mabel
please come back.
I have a plan.

love Henrietta

I fold it up in this shape

and then I throw it out into the night.

'What are you throwing that out there for?'
says Mabel.

'Mabel, I wish you wouldn't just appear
and disappear like that. It's very hard to make
plans for someone who is unpredictable.'

'But I'm busy preparing for the annual

Big Bunch of Small Creatures Ball.

Bendle Bristlemouth will be there,
of course, so I'm practising
my moves and collecting
my potions.'

'Well, I gather you already
know my plan for Uncle George,
so I'm not going to tell you.'

I say it a little bit huffily,
because it's quite
annoying dealing with a fairy who
knows your secret thoughts and
has read your secret letter even before
you've sent it out into the sky.

The great thing about O.H. is that we talk about
things and work things out together. Whereas
Mabel seems to know everything already.

Mabel must be listening to my thoughts again,
because she floats over and lands on my shoulder.
Then she kisses me on the cheek and says,
'Thank you for helping me. I'm very grateful.
And if you don't want me to listen to your
thoughts, just put your hands over your ears.
Then I won't be able to hear them.'
She jumps down, folds her wings in
and wriggles into the sock.

I hop into bed and put my hands over my ears.
But I forget to keep them there because
just as I wonder what the

Big Bunch of Small Creatures Ball is,

a small silver envelope flies in the window.
Inside there's an invitation.

Henrietta P. Hoppenbeek
is invited to the
Big Bunch
of
Small Creatures Ball

WHERE: The doorway on Thistle Lane
WHEN: November Full Moon
TIME: The Quiet Hour

Suddenly I feel very excited. Imagine me,
Henrietta P. Hoppenbeek the First, at the

Big Bunch of Small Creatures Ball

I'm squirming and wriggling in bed because
the idea of it is just too squirmingly good,
when Mabel calls up from her sock.
'And in case you're wondering,
the key is for the doorway on Thistle Lane.
Now please stop wriggling and go to sleep.
Otherwise you'll be too tired for the ball.'

Uncle George and I are out walking,
as that is what Uncle George likes to do
when he's wearing a new hat.
Mabel is very well installed inside it.
There's a little ledge for her to sit on
and two holes so that she can see out.
Unfortunately, Olive Higgie is at the dentist,
which is a terrible place to be,
and I'm feeling very sorry for her.

'Uncle George,' I say.
'What kind of a lady do you
like to fall in love with?'

large ones   small ones   loud ones

'Well, you know me. My problem is I fall in love
with all the ladies – big ones, small ones, loud ones,
quiet ones, fancy ones, plain ones, messy ones, neat
ones, serious ones, funny ones, relaxed ones, bossy
ones and… Well, actually, that's not quite true.
I'm not keen on the bossy ones.'

quiet ones   fancy ones   plain ones

Mabel whispers, 'Can you ask him to be more specific, please?'

So I say, 'Uncle George, just say that I had fallen in love with someone and I wanted that someone to ask me to a dance. What should I do to make him ask me?'

Uncle George tips the hat and whistles,
and Mabel nearly falls out.
Then he says,
in a very serious
grown-up tone,
'Well, Henrietta,
the best thing to do
is to be yourself.
After many long years
in the business of love,
I have discovered
that the most lovable lady
is one who is not afraid
to be true to herself.
It's not so easy.
People are always trying
to impress each other.
But I always *always*
fall in love with someone
who isn't trying too hard
to impress me.

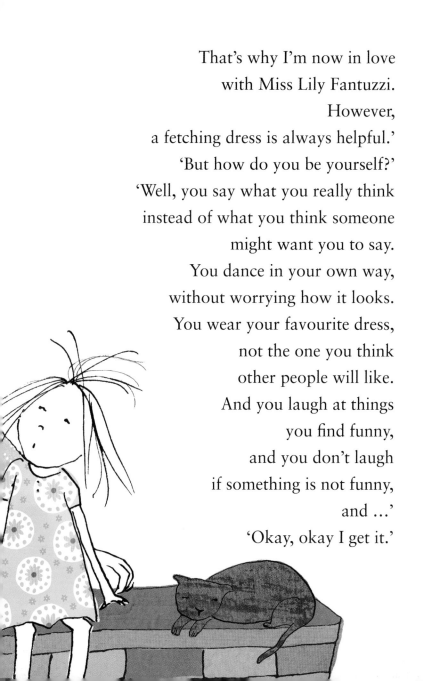

That's why I'm now in love
with Miss Lily Fantuzzi.
However,
a fetching dress is always helpful.'
'But how do you be yourself?'
'Well, you say what you really think
instead of what you think someone
might want you to say.
You dance in your own way,
without worrying how it looks.
You wear your favourite dress,
not the one you think
other people will like.
And you laugh at things
you find funny,
and you don't laugh
if something is not funny,
and ...'
'Okay, okay I get it.'

Uncle George has a sunny look on his face, as if he's feeling all smoochy just thinking about love. Then he stops suddenly and says, 'How odd, I just felt the hat lift off my head.'

Mabel flies off with a sparkling grin on her face, doing big loops in the sky as she goes.

I wonder if Uncle George almost believes in something, because it looks as if he's watching her go. Then he laughs and picks me up and puts me on his shoulders. 'Anyway, Henrietta, you're already an absolute being-yourself-expert, so all I'd say to you is don't go changing for anyone.'

The Big Bunch of Small Creatures Ball

It's midnight and Mabel and I are off to the ball.
Mabel is wearing her favourite dress,
which is green, of course, with spots.
I'm wearing my favourite dress,
which is red, of course, with yellow flowers.
I'm also wearing Uncle George's hat,
because he forgot to take it home
and I think the hat deserves
to come to the ball.
Mabel has a crown of dandelions.

'Mabel, will I be too big for
the ball?'

'You'll be the biggest
creature there. Isn't
that something?'

'I guess so. Who else
will be there?'

'Oody oody, wait and see.'
Mabel sits on my shoulder
and flutters her wings.

61

The doorway on Thistle Lane is not at all like
the entrance to a ball. Long weeds scrounge
around the bottom, and a web of ivy wriggles up
the face of it. But then I notice that the keyhole is
glowing and pulsing with silver light.

It makes me feel all fizzy inside, and I can tell
Mabel is feeling all fluttery too,
because her wings don't stop moving.
I put the silver key in the lock and slowly,
slowly push open the door.

Lordy Lordy, what a sight.

It's a big room with crumbly old stone walls and no roof. The sky is all lit up with stars and swishes of moving lights.

'They're fireflies,' whispers Mabel.

There are fairies everywhere, darting and hovering.

And elves dancing and stomping and singing, holding hands and flinging their legs up and weaving through the crowd in big circles. In the middle, a group of small folk play fiddles and bells. A fat little elf with a white beard and a curly green hat hoots as he bangs a tyre with a drumstick.

The music is fast and loud and it almost feels like a wave that might take you up and whirl you around.

'Dance, then, if you want to,' sings Mabel. 'Come on.' She floats off into the air and does a beautiful swirl.

I watch the butterflies and dragonflies and ladybirds buzzing about in the air. Everyone is so delicate and small that I feel a bit shy, for once in my life. I take off my hat and squish myself down to be as small as possible, which is quite uncomfortable.

Just as I am watching two ladybirds playing leap-frog with a dragonfly, a fairy falls from the sky and lands on her bottom right in front of me. I jump up to see if she is all right but, before I even take a step, a bird lands on my shoulder and whispers, 'Never help a fairy who's fallen from the sky. It only hurts their pride to fall. It doesn't hurt their bottoms.'

'Oh,' I say, as if it's perfectly normal to have a bird telling you what to do, though actually I feel strange and giddy and excited.

'I'm Aldo, Mabel's best friend. Henrietta, I presume?' says the bird.

'That's right. Henrietta the great go-getter.'

'The great go-getter indeed. Well, shall we go get a good time then? Mabel has charged me to look after you while she's engaged in Bendle Bristlemouth's tedious shenanigans.'

Aldo sighs and points his wing to the corner
of the room.

A circle of fairies sit at the feet of a red-cheeked elf, who is busy laughing and gesturing and pointing all at once.

Mabel is gazing up at him.

'What are they doing?' I ask Aldo, since I'm not sure what 'tedious shenanigans' are.

'Oh, the little love-struck twits just sit there while Bendle thinks up naughty pranks and then watches as they do his mischief for him. Look at that fairy dangling a silk thread over the nose of that poor old elf.

Aldo swoops over and plucks the silk thread
out of the fairy's hand, as the old elf
is sniffing and sneezing.
'Aldo,' I say seriously. 'Surely
Mabel isn't a twit?'
'Mabel is usually a very smart fairy,
but love does strange things to us all.
It looks like she is next in line, too.
Oh, dear me. Shall we dance, Henrietta?'
'Oh no, I can't dance here.
I'm too big. I'd be embarrassed.
And anyway, shouldn't we
help Mabel?'
'Remember the rule
of the fallen fairy.
You can't help a fairy.
Not unless she asks you to.'

Mabel did ask me to help. But I don't really feel like helping her to win over Bendle Bristlemouth, I feel like helping her to lose him. But if that's not technically allowed, then what can I do?

'Dance!' says a voice from below my knees. It's a ragged little elf whose curly hair seems to be shining, or is it his eyes shining? He winks and then runs off, doing cartwheels, leaping and throwing his arms around wildly. I make myself small again and try to dance just like a fairy, delicately, in the manner of a flower, but it isn't any fun at all. The shining-eyed elf is laughing and I think of Uncle George, with the shine in his eyes.

Suddenly I know how to help Mabel.

I dance the Henrietta P. Hoppenbeek Dance, wild and wide, spinning and leaping. And I don't care that I'm different from everyone else here. I dance just how I want to dance.

I see bats swooping and silkworms glowing and birds darting and dark misty lake bugs scuttling, and then I see Mabel hovering right in front of my nose, frowning.

She says, 'Henrietta, oh dear, Bendle has told me to trip you up and make a fool of you.'

'But there's no need, Mabel. I'm making a fool of myself and it's great fun.'

Mabel stops very still in the air and looks at me in a perplexed way. Slowly she starts grinning, and then laughing.

She whispers to me, 'Henrietta, isn't it something to be the biggest creature here?'

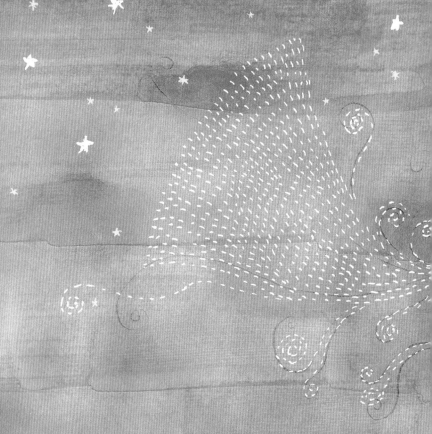

She whirls her wonderful circles as I wave my wild
laughing arms and together we are dancing and
looping and leaping for joy. And then Aldo joins us,
and so does the elf with the shining eyes.
Soon there's a whole circle of creatures whirling
around me.

We all spin and spin until we can't spin anymore,

and then we fall in a pile and gaze up at the stars.

Soon it's just Mabel and me and Aldo and the shining-eyed elf – whose name is Melo – sitting in a circle on the grass. We have been talking and drinking mulberry juice out of gumnut cups. Around us the party is beginning to quieten down, the music is slow and some creatures are leaving.

I notice that Mabel and Melo are holding hands and smiling at each other, just like Uncle George does when he's in love.

'Aldo,' I say dreamily. 'I think it's time for me to go home now. Would you show me the way?'

'I'd be delighted,' says Aldo.

We wave goodbye
to Mabel and Melo,
and as we wander home
I ask Aldo if he thinks
they are in love.

'Who knows?'

'Yes, who knows?'
I say philosophically,
because I would never
have known that
the last piece of
chocolate ripple cake
could lead to a
Big Bunch of
Small Creatures Ball.
And now I do.

Waking up

Next morning, I hear Albert talking to himself, in Albert language. Dad is singing in the shower, 'You are my sunshine my only sunshine, you make me happy when pies are gay.' I leap out of bed and look in the sock, but Mabel isn't there.

Albert is happy to see me though, and I do particularly care about Albert after all. He stands up in his cot and says, 'Al awake now.'

'Albert, there's something I have to tell you about growing up.'

Albert repeats, 'Al awake now.'

'Albert, listen. This is important information. Be very careful not to become one of those grown-ups who think that certain things aren't really real, like sea monsters and martians, and stars that guide you, and wishes that come true, and lands ruled by lost socks, and creatures that need to laugh. And also, it's much better to give the last piece of cake to someone else than to eat it yourself.'

Albert bangs the cot with his hand and says, 'Up now.' So I gather he's got the message.

Anyway, just talking about stars and wishes and creatures makes me feel all excited about the day and all the discoveries I might make.

I throw on my most splendid dress, and just as I'm about to hoon out the door to tell O.H. all about the ball, another envelope comes zigzagging in the window.

Dear Henrietta,

Thank you for letting me sleep in your sock.
Thank you especially for helping me lose
Bendle Bristlemouth
and find Melo Merrytoe.
I am very pleased to know you.
Aldo thinks you are the very very finest
dancing partner. I do too.
Bye bye, or as we fairies say, eye bye
(which means: look out for me, I'll be nearby).
Love Mabel
P.S. Melo and I are eating honey
on the wild white plains of Peasebury.

I'm not sure, but maybe I also hear a little giggle and some humming wings, but it might just be my imagination. Dad says I have a very healthy one.